FRUITCAKE AND FELONIES

A BELLE HARBOR COZY MYSTERY (BOOK 13)

SUE HOLLOWELL

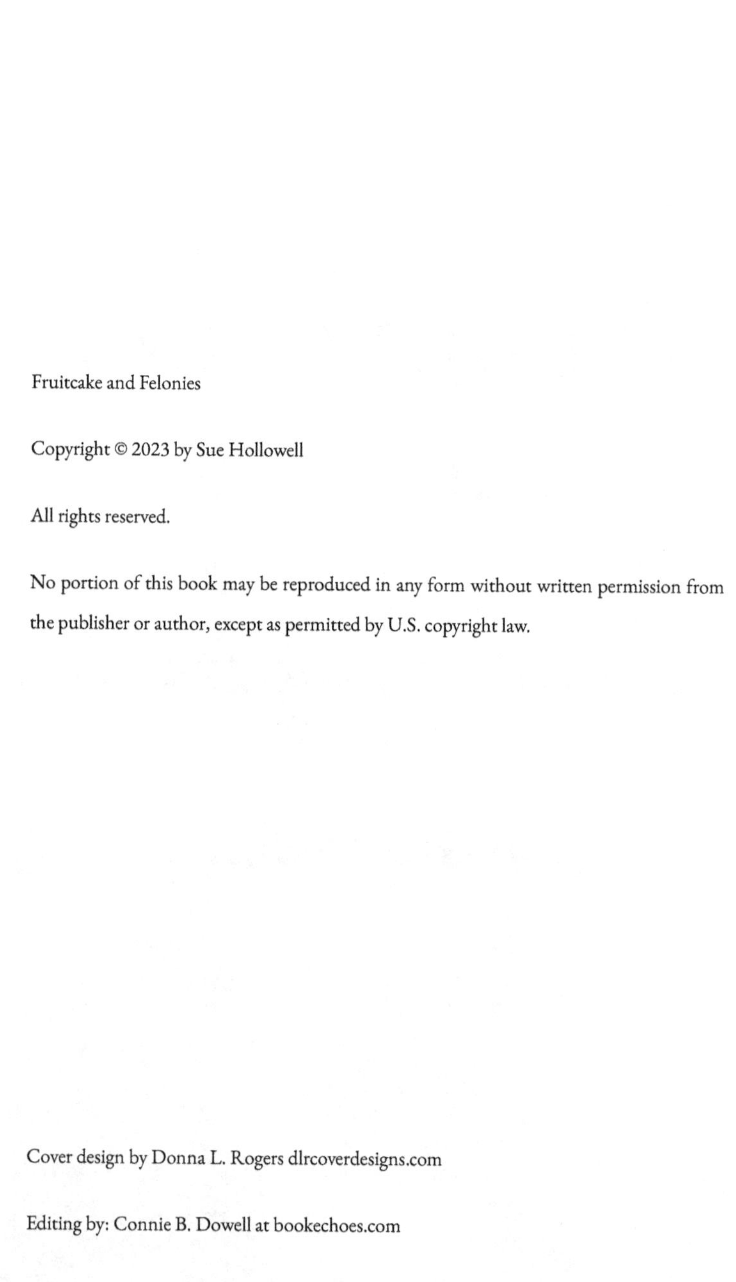

Fruitcake and Felonies

Copyright © 2023 by Sue Hollowell

All rights reserved.

No portion of this book may be reproduced in any form without written permission from the publisher or author, except as permitted by U.S. copyright law.

Cover design by Donna L. Rogers dlrcoverdesigns.com

Editing by: Connie B. Dowell at bookechoes.com

CONTENTS

CHAPTER ONE

"This is insane, and pretty awesome," Linda said, as we entered the main room at the convention center.

She nailed it. We stopped inside the door to the main gaming room and ogled the wall in front of us. The center of it held the main projection screen, which must have spanned twenty feet long by ten feet high. On both sides of that were several smaller screens, still enormous in their own right. The seating area held rows of incredibly comfy-looking chairs the players would use as they competed for the top prize in the competition. The soft brown cushions beckoned me for a nap. I expected the din from the group tomorrow wouldn't allow that. Between the chairs, a wooden table would hold the food and drinks for the players.

Our adorable teenage baker Dexter had been prepping for this competition for an entire year.

I moved to the front of the room and plopped into a chair in the center of the row. I sank inches into the plush and gazed at the screen. The players on the screen would be larger than life. Dexter had regaled us with stories about the football video game he and his friends enjoyed playing, Gridiron Gash. While I was no stranger to sports, and had a brother playing professional baseball, I didn't have a chance to keep up with Dexter's play-by-play. Though the energy of his detailed descriptions, and the spark in his eye, jazzed me up to watch a few rounds when the games began.

Linda plunked into the chair to my right, whispering, "Insane."

"Thank you for agreeing to help. I actually have no idea what to expect." Scooting forward, I craned my neck around the room. "I can only imagine the gamers will gobble up everything we offer them." I'd seen with Dexter and heard that teenage boys eat you out of house and home. If my brother was any indication, I doubted we would have enough to last the duration of the tournament.

"Of course," Linda said. "I agree. We won't be packing up any leftovers after this."

"If I haven't said it recently, I'm so glad we hired Noah for the bakery."

With Linda's recent marriage to my Uncle Jack, I predicted her time at *Luna's Bakery and Cafe* would diminish. Her partnership, and exceptional baking skills, had catapulted my business success. But to be fair, I wanted her and Unkie to spend all the time together that they wanted. Noah's presence gave me a great excuse to encourage that. Now, to get Uncle Jack to slow down from his antique business. But that was another conversation for another day.

"Can you imagine how rowdy this place will be when they get rolling?" I could almost feel the energy.

Linda stood. "We should probably get back to the setup."

I hoisted myself out of the chair and rubbed my sweaty hands on my apron. Nerves were not from this catering job. My boyfriend's parents were arriving, and my anxiety about meeting them was through the roof. Justin insisted they would love me. I hoped so.

We stopped outside the gaming room and Linda quickly squeezed me and looked me directly in the eye. She grabbed both of my clammy hands and firmly said, "They will love you. But even if they don't, Justin does. And that's all that matters."

Yeah, but how would that relationship go if my boyfriend's parents didn't like me? Justin was drama-free. But if there were tension every time his parents and I were together... I couldn't go there. I would do my best and let the chips fall where they may. Easier said than done. I was still a recovering people pleaser.

"You're right, but still." Turning my attention to the task at hand, Linda and I returned to our booth. I glanced around the rest of the food court. Several stations provided hand-held savory options. The gamers would have choices of pizza slices, pigs-in-a-blanket, bite-sized quiches, taquitos, and so much more. My stomach churned just pondering all the gut bombs. "There should be a booth with just antacids."

"I feel the same way. How do those kids do it?"

I reached for one of the boxes on a cart of supplies we had wheeled in. Finger foods were the name of the game for this gig. We had baked hundreds of mini-cupcakes, tiny tarts, baby donuts, and brownies. Removing the display boxes, we laid them out on the table. Each one had a cover and a lock. I had seriously debated whether leaving everything overnight was safe. But the conference head had committed to all the vendors that our booths would be secure. It was the only logical choice, as the gamers would start at o-dark-thirty. There would be no time to set up on day one of the competition.

We continued unpacking and loading all the treats into the cases. Special for this event, I had ordered some disposable paper cups and funnels to make it easier to transport the goodies. It was the best I could do to minimize the stickiness of the sweets on the game controllers. One booth down the aisle was nothing but cleaning supplies. They had provided each of us a bucket of wet wipes to offer each gamer.

"I'm here," Florence announced, heading toward us, carrying a tray with mini-bundt cakes.

I whipped my head toward Linda, hoping for clarity on this surprise visit from the bookstore owner. Florence's and my relationship was a work in progress. For many reasons. Linda shrugged.

"OK, dear. Where should I put these?" Florence gazed along our display table.

Straightening up, I gathered my thoughts. Why was she here with some type of bakery item at my booth for the video game competition?

"Hi, Florence," was all I got out. *C'mon brain. Figure out what's going on!*

She set her tray down on the table and scooted two of my display cases apart. "They can go right here."

Her brown little mini-cakes sat in ruffled papers. They were bursting with what appeared to be fruit and nuts. Did she actually bring fruitcake to an event attended mostly by teenagers and young adults?

"What are these?" I picked one up and rotated it in my hand. Yep, fruitcake. I couldn't imagine even the hungriest would partake. While they were adorable in the paper cups, there was no disguising the gummy lumps of clay.

"These are my specialty. You're not the only one who can bake." Florence sniffed and lifted her nose in the air.

Linda approached and asked, "May I try one?"

"Of course," Florence said and handed it to her.

Unwrapping it, Linda grabbed a napkin and split it into two pieces, handing one to me. She widened her eyes and bravely took a big bite. Nothing like diving in. "Ohhh, Florence. This is fantastic."

Florence leaned in with her hand cupped to the side of her mouth. "I don't use that horrific candied fruit. It's all fresh."

Linda nodded and finished the last bite.

Following suit, I bit into the cake, discovering an unexpected delight. My mind reeled, trying to remember if a conversation with Florence about her fruitcake had just slipped my mind. It was certainly possible given all I had going on. Next task at hand, come up with a name that wasn't fruitcake to convince the kids to eat them. I plopped the remaining bite into my mouth. "Mmmm."

Florence grinned.

"Tilly!" Lanky, curly-haired Dexter rushed in.

CHAPTER TWO

We all spun to greet him. His curls sprang in a variety of directions, as if he had just gotten out of bed. His t-shirt had several wrinkles and stains dotting the front.

"Dexter," I said, moving out from behind the display table. His focus on this tournament had been maniacal in recent weeks. The grand prize was one hundred thousand dollars. And they would create the winner as a prominent character in one of the game maker's upcoming new releases.

"Uh, hi," he replied, scanning the room. He looked down and smoothed his hands over his shirt. Lifting his head, he blushed. "I guess I didn't get a clean shirt this morning."

I could understand his distraction because of the game, but his demeanor was above and beyond a normal amount of excitement.

"Are you OK?" I reached out my hand and touched his arm to get his attention.

He jerked his head toward me. "What?"

Grabbing his hand, I pulled him into our booth and guided him toward a chair.

Plopping down hard, he ran his hand through his tousled hair, causing more of it to jut out.

I kneeled in front of him, grabbing his hands and looking directly into his eyes. "Dexter, I think you need to take a break. You're wearing yourself out."

Furiously shaking his head, the curls flew side-to-side. "I can't."

"If you don't, you won't be in any shape for the competition."

Linda approached Dexter from the side and placed a hand on his shoulder. Glancing up at her, he nodded. "OK. I can take a small break and go home to check on my mom." Turning his attention back to me, he continued. "Then I have to get back here." He stood.

When this tournament was over, I hoped he would relax a bit. The time he spent on the game was concerning to me. But the main experience I had with teenage boys was my brother. Maybe Dexter's behavior was more typical than I was accustomed to.

"There's the superstar." A man not much older than the teenage gamers strolled up to my booth. Except for his name tag announcing

Kenneth as Tournament Director, he could have been mistaken for one of the youths in the competition. There didn't appear to be much variation in the demographic of people entered into the game.

Dexter bolted from the chair, beaming. "You think so?"

"Yep. I think you have a real shot this year," Kenneth said.

Grinning ear-to-ear, Dexter said, "Did you hear that, Tilly?"

With all my heart, I hoped he did well. Even if he didn't win, he could still get a prize.

"I've seen your preliminary games, and you've definitely improved from last year," Kenneth said.

With Kenneth's encouragement, I expected Dexter to double down on his efforts for the home stretch. That grand prize was now in his sights. I made a vow to keep a close eye on him the next couple of days to make sure he was taking enough breaks and getting proper nourishment. He still had a long way to go. The competition was double-elimination. Even if he lost in one round, he would continue to play unless he lost a second time. Several months before the finals this weekend, he and his friends had to compete to qualify.

Patting Dexter on the back, Kenneth said, "This guy is an up-and-coming player. I expect great things this year."

Somehow, it seemed this gaming had developed from a fun pastime to a full-time job. Was that really a thing these days?

A woman who appeared about my age rushed in and stopped next to Kenneth, whispering something into his ear.

He bent his head toward her, furrowing his brows, his face turning ashen.

She quietly said, "Yes."

Kenneth straightened up and looked around. The other food vendors were equally hard at work prepping for the onslaught of players very early tomorrow as the tournament officially began. He mumbled, "We don't have a choice. We have to shut it down."

Dexter began pacing in front of our booth. What level of tragedy would shut down this epic event? Dexter wrung his hands, his head bowed.

Kenneth instructed his assistant, "Please make an announcement that nobody is to leave until instructed otherwise by the authorities."

She agreed and scurried out of the room.

"What do you mean, I can't leave?" Florence piped up. She had completely unloaded her cakes front and center of my table. I had full intention of moving them to the back after she had left. While Linda and I found them tasty, I was still skeptical they would be well-received by the masses.

"I'm sorry, ma'am," Kenneth said. "There's an issue the police need to resolve before we can let everyone go."

Marching to meet Kenneth face-to-face, she said, "I'll have you know that the chief of police is my beau."

Taking a step back, Kenneth said, "I hope this won't take long. But I can't let anyone go until I'm authorized."

Florence whipped a cell phone out of her pocket and began texting. I suspected if the police had already been called, Barney was en route.

"Can you share what's happened?" Linda asked.

"Well, I guess it's probably all over social media by now." Kenneth heaved a massive sigh. On the cusp of a tournament with record-breaking prizes, there was what appeared to be a major issue. I fully expected him to divulge a theft. The cost of the electronics at this event must have run well into six figures. I couldn't see how they would secure everything to prevent them from disappearing.

Kenneth stared at our antsy teenager and said, "I'm sorry. But Caden was found strangled in the practice room."

Florence squealed. Dexter abruptly stopped and stared at Kenneth. Caden wasn't a name I heard often from Dexter, so I didn't think it was one of his close friends.

Dexter funneled his hand through his curls, prompting most of them to stand. He furtively glanced in my direction.

"Oh, Dexter," I said.

"But," he started. Staring at me, he continued, "Tilly, I didn't..."

I stepped into Dexter's path and spread my arms for a hug. His eyes glazed over. He opened and closed his mouth without a sound. I squeezed him hard and clasped his hand.

"Let's go someplace a little more quiet," I suggested. As long as we didn't leave the building, I figured we were within the rules.

"I have to go," Kenneth said, and sped away.

"Linda and Florence, can you take care of the booth for a bit?" With a death on the premises, there was no way they would begin the competition on schedule. We would have to pack up all of our stuff and return it to the bakery. My customers would be in for an epic sale.

I tugged on Dexter's arm to prod him. Reluctantly, he followed my lead.

CHAPTER THREE

As we stepped into the hallway, we encountered small groups huddled and muttering to each other. Leading Dexter along the path, I glanced into each room to find one that was vacant. I peeled off and turned to ensure he followed. I closed the door behind us to muddle the voices from the hall. Dexter stood just inside the room, head lowered.

"Dexter," I attempted to lure him out of his shock. He didn't budge. More quietly, I repeated his name.

"Hmm?" He glanced up and around the room as if he wondered how we had transported here from the food court.

I sat in one chair and patted the one next to me, turning mine to face it.

He ambled over and dropped down, his hands wringing between his knees. With tears in his eyes, he repeated, "Tilly, I didn't."

Where did I even start to comfort him while quizzing to find out more? "Did you know Caden?"

Lifting his shoulders in a shrug, he let them drop and said, "Yeah."

OK. One-word answers wouldn't get us anywhere. "Was he one of your friends?" I prodded as gently as I could.

Dexter's head popped up. His eyes shot daggers at me.

I moved my chair back and held out my hand. So, no. This was getting me nowhere. It was only a matter of time before the police arrived and quizzed Dexter. If he was uncomfortable answering my questions, the interrogation would push him over the edge. "I'm so sorry, Dexter. The police will also have these questions."

He bolted from his chair and paced. Our chill and easy-going teenager was beside himself. Halting, he said, "Caden won the tournament last year."

Well, that explained a few things. He was the one to beat for the record-breaking prize.

Standing up, I pondered if I would have to pace with Dexter to keep the conversation going. "Ah, so he was the one to beat."

"Yeah, except-" Dexter started and glanced around as if to see if anyone else was listening in. He leaned forward and through gritted teeth, he said, "That scum ball cheated. And everyone knew it."

How in the world could you cheat at something like this, especially when everyone was watching you on a big screen? Was this just sour grapes? I believed Dexter thought Caden cheated, but did he know for certain?

He continued, "I'm sure you don't believe me. But Tommy saw him using cheat codes."

The volume of voices from the hall escalated, leading me to conclude the police had arrived and were wrangling everyone to get witness statements. My private time with Dexter was quickly ending.

He pounded his fist on his thigh. "I really needed to win the prize this year." No doubt the money would be life changing for him and his family. Dexter was the oldest of three kids being raised by a single mom. She worked housekeeping at a local bed-and-breakfast and did her best with what she had. "Caden didn't deserve it, and we wanted to make sure he didn't win this year."

Oh, boy. That kind of talk would land him in a heap of trouble. "Dexter."

He held out his hand, seeming to come to his senses. "I know, Tilly."

But did he? I could only go so far to protect him before this catapulted out of my hands. In my heart, there was no way this young man could hurt another human being. But in the heat of the moment, would he have lost his temper? Was there an accident? I had to further probe while I had the opportunity, no matter how uncomfortable it made him.

"When was the last time you saw Caden?"

Dexter tilted his head, peering at the ceiling. "Yeah, I saw him with Tommy in the practice room." He paused. "Huh."

We didn't have much more time. "What, Dexter?"

"They had their heads together. And when I came up to them, Tommy acted all nervous. Like there was something going on he didn't want me to see."

The door squeaked open, and we both jumped. Barney poked his head in. "Tilly?" He glanced at Dexter and stepped into the room, swinging the door fully open.

I was busted. But Barney knew better than to expect me not to ask questions. "Hi, Barney."

Dexter sidled up to me, and I quickly squeezed his arm. We waited for instructions.

Barney clucked his tongue. "OK. Right now, we're just getting everyone's contact info and asking them to come back at specific times tomorrow for interviews."

"Tilly?" Dexter said.

"It's OK, Dexter. They just want to find out what happened." I was certain Barney wouldn't let me be present when Dexter was questioned. He would be fine if he just stuck to the facts. No embellishment of his feelings for Caden. Of his innocence, I was confident. His friends? Not so sure. This investigation might take some turns that would change his future. But we needed to let the evidence lead the way.

A tall, large man entered the room. "Oh, sorry to interrupt, chief," he said.

"Nah. We're done, Ian," Barney said to him, writing in his notebook. "Dexter, tomorrow at 10." He pointed his pencil in Dexter's direction.

Ian approached Dexter with a hug. "Sorry, bro. This really sucks." Ian sniffed and wiped the moisture from his eyes on his sleeve.

"Yeah," Dexter responded with some type of bro handshake.

Pointing at Dexter, Ian continued, "This guy here is an up and comer. My bets were on him to win it all this year."

"You'll have to wait and see if that's possible," Barney interjected.

Dexter leaned into Ian as if they were family. "This guy is the sponsor," Dexter informed me. "And this is my boss, Tilly." Dexter gestured toward me.

"Nice to meet you Ian, even if these are horrible circumstances," I said.

Turning to face Dexter, Ian grabbed him by the shoulders. "You hang in there. My money's on you. Caden didn't deserve to win, especially with those cheating rumors swirling around him."

If the sponsor putting up that much money was concerned about Caden winning, to what extent might they go to get the person they want to win? If Dexter won, how would he be beholden to Ian and the company? Was the money going to be worth the sacrifices he might have to make for it?

I glanced at Barney, who stood back and observed this interaction. He kept his exceptional poker face. I knew he had just added Ian to his list of suspects. Anytime money was involved as a plausible motive for a crime, you were likely close to solving it if you could trace the trail to the source. And Ian had one hundred thousand reasons he might have an interest in the tournament's outcome.

"Dexter, we should probably get you home," I said.

He nodded and joined me as we exited the room. Once in the hallway, I shook out my arms to rid my body of the icky feeling I had from meeting Ian. Maybe he was just a slimy salesman. Maybe more.

But either way, I wanted Dexter away from his influence.

CHAPTER FOUR

I quickly plopped into my living room chair, cuddling with my little Peanut. She was quickly growing from the little fur ball I had recently adopted. Closing my eyes, I consumed her warmth and soft purr. She was evidence that even the crustiest of people could come together over troubles. Though I didn't know if Florence would completely forgive Justin for allowing his cat to mate with hers. We all cherished the litter that resulted, but Florence was overly protective of her Gwinnie.

"Well, little one. I need to get ready to go." I placed her on the floor, and she trotted behind me to the bedroom. Pulling open my closet door, I scanned the outfits. Living in a temperate climate meant I had little variation in the type of clothing. I retrieved a floral swing dress and held it in front of me in the mirror. If I wore some low rise boots instead of my usual Converse, that would fancy it up. Tossing the dress on the bed, I wiped my sweaty hands on my shorts. Peanut hopped up onto the bed and flopped onto my dress.

Justin had arranged a meeting with his parents at Fiona's. They were in town for a week to visit from Arizona. He assured me they would love me, but I couldn't help being nervous. Peanut meowed as I moved her from the dress. With the boots added to the look, I looked a little more presentable than my normal attire. "Well, little one." I gave her a final pet. "I can't delay any longer." She sent me off with another meow.

I parked in a lot near the restaurant. The short walk allowed me to combat some of my anxiety. I shook out my hands as I rounded the corner to enter Fiona's. Every table and booth in the place was filled. I inhaled as I scanned the room to find Justin.

Fiona scurried over to me. "Tilly," she said and hugged me. She held my left hand and looked me straight in the eyes. "They're going to love you." Everyone kept repeating that phrase, and I hoped it would come true.

Shaking my head, I chuckled. "Is it that obvious?"

"I know you. Ever since Justin announced his parents' visit, you've been wondering how you can present yourself to them." She nailed it. Justin deserved someone that his parents also approved of. I didn't want to be the one to come between them. She looked me up and down. "And you couldn't look any cuter."

My shoulders eased down. She knew how to relieve my anxiousness. The stress of the day still boiled underneath my veneer. I really wanted to huddle up with Justin to get his thoughts on the death of Caden. But for now, I needed to move that subject to the back of my mind. Maybe it could percolate in the recesses and come up with an epiphany during dinner.

Fiona squeezed and released my hand as we approached the table. Justin and his dad stood, Justin pulling out my chair.

"Palomas all around," Fiona said. Her signature cocktail was a favorite of mine. And a drink might tranquilize me just enough to have a normal conversation.

Justin scooted in my chair as I sat, giving me a kiss on the cheek. "Mom, Dad, this is Tilly." He beamed at me. Oh, I loved that man for so many reasons.

Justin's mom quickly looked at her watch, but not subtly enough for me not to notice. I was ten minutes later than the time Justin had told me.

"I'm so sorry I'm late. It's nice to finally meet you," I said, acknowledging my tardiness, hoping that would shift me into their good graces.

Justin waved me off. "Tilly, these are my parents, Patricia and Albert."

Albert rose a bit from his chair and smiled at me. Patricia glanced at Justin and back at me, half smiling.

Fiona arrived with our drinks. It was all I could do not to guzzle it. I took a small sip through the straw, feeling the liquid cooling my throat. OK. I could do this.

"What have you been doing since you arrived in Belle Harbor?" I asked. Maybe I could offer a good recommendation for an activity they might like.

"Well, Justin whisked us here as soon as we arrived," Patricia said. She glanced at her watch again. Wow, she didn't really seem to want to be here.

"Do you have any plans yet?" I asked Justin. He reached my hand under the table and squeezed.

A loud crash came from the kitchen as I imagined a tray of plates hitting the floor. Patricia jumped and placed her hand over her heart, looking at Albert. I needed to pace myself, but I grabbed a gulp of my drink. With the place packed, and the music playing, the volume made it a little challenging to have much of a dinner conversation. I had hoped familiar territory would give me a leg up on the meeting of Justin's parents. Now I was rethinking the venue. We might have to try another, quieter restaurant for me to redeem myself.

"Wow, it's noisy in here," Patricia said.

"So, Mom. I thought you might like to go to Tilly's uncle's antique shop," Justin offered.

"That sounds very nice, dear," she replied, warmly smiling at her son.

If anyone could smooth things over with Justin's parents, it would be Uncle Jack. Picking up my glass, it was over half empty. Would two drinks before dinner be too much? What was the etiquette when meeting the boyfriend's parents?

Patricia lifted her glass and said, "These are superb." OK. Maybe my strategy would be to just keep pace with her.

Fiona arrived, facing me from across the table. She was staring me down, I'm sure attempting to impart some peace in response to what she must have seen was a very strained facial expression. Did she know about Caden's death? The small town, coupled with social media, usually meant word traveled at lightning speed. She took our food order and promised a return with another round of drinks.

Patricia sucked on her straw, slurping the last bit of her drink. She looked up at us and giggled.

"I'd love to show you my bakery, if you have time," I offered.

"Maybe," Patricia replied with a wave of her hand.

Two servers arrived with both our second round of drinks and our food. I hoped my favorite menu item of smoked macaroni and cheese would provide the promised comfort. For the next several minutes, the conversation stopped, and we all focused on the plate in front of us. I peeked at Justin to my left. He dove into his dinner like nothing was wrong. Was I being hyper-sensitive to his parents' reception of me? From everything Justin had shared, they were very loving. He said they had been looking forward to meeting me. Beyond the obligatory niceties, how did they really feel?

"Tilly, is everything OK?" Albert asked.

Lifting my head, I realized I hadn't taken a bite, only moved the food around in the bowl. "Oh, yes," I said. But it wasn't all right. Not only was the dinner a downer, Dexter was embroiled in the death of a fellow gamer. I really needed a do over for the day.

CHAPTER FIVE

"Good morning, beautiful." My phone buzzed as I headed down the boardwalk to Unkie's Checkered Past Antiques. My smile widened and my face warmed as I read Justin's text, hoping I kept that feeling about him for the rest of my life. That was the best way to start my day. I juggled my coffee with my phone.

"Lol. Good Morning." The cool morning air brushing my face assisted the caffeine in waking me up. Another restless night. Dexter moped through his tasks at the bakery this morning. I knew he would rather be at the tournament, competing against others for that grand prize. Not only was the event delayed, the death was someone that Dexter knew. It took everything I had to not grill him. After he talked with Barney, I would circle back with Dexter to make sure he was OK. And, of course, to find out what he said. There was just no way he was involved. Though he had an obvious motive, with what the winnings from the competition could do for his future.

I dropped my phone, attempting to read Justin's next text. Stopping and leaning against the wall, I inhaled. Literally and figuratively juggling too much. Bending to get my phone, I read Justin's message. "My parents loved you. And I do too."

Really? I was certain I left a terrible impression, arriving late, distracted dinner conversation, and I was sure there were other factors. "No way. I didn't come across very well. I would like another chance."

Scooting down the wall, I sat for a minute to finish my coffee and conversation, not wanting to chance spilling something all over myself.

"You're too hard on yourself. Gotta go. Love you."

Holding the phone to my chest, I gazed into the rolling waves approaching the shore. Yes, I was. A recovering perfectionist with high responsibility as one of my strengths. My identity had always been the good student, good daughter, good employee. And when I messed up, I felt like a disappointment to others. Nobody was ever as hard on me as I was on myself.

I hoisted myself from the pavement for the last stretch to Unkie's, tucking my phone into my pocket. My morning was about to get even better. Visiting Uncle Jack always picked me up. He was my biggest cheerleader. I still had to pinch myself often that I had gotten so lucky with Unkie's support for my dream. He had carved out a corner of his antique shop for my fledgling bakery not that long ago. If not for his encouragement, I certainly wouldn't be where I was with Luna's Cafe and Bakery. A legacy to both him and my Grandma Luna.

Entering the bright room, Unkie and Carlos were busy unboxing new arrivals. He kept the inventory rotating with new items all the time. His customers appreciated the excitement they had with new finds. And Uncle Jack always had a backstory to tell for most of the antiques. I approached them at the back of the store. "Hi, guys."

"Hi, Tilly," Carlos said.

Unkie greeted me with a quick hug and peck on the cheek. He moved the stray hair from the front of my eyes and tilted his head.

I could read his face. Waving my hand, I said, "I'm fine."

He shook his head. "Not buying it."

"You're right. But I have a lot going on."

Unkie gestured to the back of the store, where he maintained a small coffee corner with a table and chairs. One of his favorite places to chat up anyone who would have a conversation with him. His coffee chats were almost as legendary as his antique items.

"I met Albert and Patricia," he said.

Bolting up from the chair, I said, "They were here already?" I had hoped to prep him with my perspective. Oh boy.

Holding up both of his hands, he took a step back. "Tilly, they were delightful." He had lowered his voice and slowed his speech.

Had I been overly sensitive last night to their reception of me? I was severely distracted from the events earlier with Caden's death, and the aftermath with Dexter. Maybe I had overblown the situation.

"What did they say?" I quizzed him.

He shrugged. "Mostly how they like Belle Harbor. They enjoyed dinner last night and getting to meet you."

My confidence rose that this might work out after all. "Are you sure?"

Unkie was not one to pull punches. But he wouldn't want to hurt me either. I studied his expression to see if he was withholding something to protect my feelings.

"Tilly," he said. "Don't overthink it."

I frequently borrowed trouble that actually never arrived. My brain could catastrophize in a split second; most of the scenarios didn't materialize.

My stress eased for the time being. "OK. I'll take it at face value. Thank you."

The shop door opened to Uncle Jack's best friend and the chief of police. "Hey, you two," Barney greeted.

He held a plate in his hand, covered in plastic, that looked suspiciously like the fruitcakes from Florence. I suspected she had lots of leftovers, as I did since they had postponed the tournament.

"Hey, old man. We still on for tonight?" Uncle Jack said. They both had cars they were preparing for the annual Belle Harbor classic car show and parade. Those two motor heads could spend hours in Barney's garage tinkering. I imagined that could extend into days if we didn't periodically check on them.

Barney nodded toward Unkie and asked me, "How's Dexter?"

Shrugging, I said, "Still pretty shaken. But I hope he'll be OK, eventually. Any details you can share?"

He peeked over his shoulder and stepped forward, putting the plate on the table, and quietly said, "I can confirm it was murder. Someone strangled Caden."

"Any suspects or motive?" I probed for any news that would get Dexter off the hook.

"Everyone in the building," he said.

Of course. This crime was up close and personal. Nothing yet to ease my fears about Dexter's involvement or knowledge of the crime.

Deep down, I knew he wasn't capable. But in the heat of the moment, could he have snapped? Or was he covering for a friend?

"These are tasty cakes," Unkie said, stuffing the rest of a fruitcake into his mouth, rubbing his hands together.

"What?" I said.

Uncle Jack held one of the cakes out. "You have to try them. They aren't your typical fruitcake."

Should I confess to him that I already tried them and liked them?

"It's an old family recipe she has," Barney said. "It's real fruit instead of that chewy, candied junk."

Surprisingly, that did seem to make a big difference.

"Mmmm," Uncle Jack closed his eyes and rubbed his stomach as he popped another one into his mouth.

"Traitor," I said, grabbing one and rotating it in my hands. I couldn't figure out how she made them taste so good.

"I helped her make these," Barney said.

Unkie and I whipped our heads toward each other, eyes wide. The vision I'm sure we both had was Florence and Barney in the kitchen, Barney decked in a frilly apron. I marveled at Barney's affection for Florence. While she generally bristled toward me, he had seemed to capture her heart.

CHAPTER SIX

I nibbled a small bite with what looked like a piece of pineapple. The moisture exploded in my mouth. The taste was well beyond what these little cakes looked like. I gobbled up the rest and wiped my hands on a napkin.

"Pretty good, huh?" Barney asked, nodding his head.

Unkie was now on number three. He had completely migrated to the dark side. Yeah, they were very good.

My phone buzzed several times. I looked at the time and realized I was overdue to return to the bakery. My confidence in my new employee, Noah, was off the charts. He had managed kitchens before in large cities and was looking for something a little more laid back. His easy-going personality meshed very well with Linda and me, and he had voluntarily assumed mentoring for Dexter. However, that was no excuse to leave him on his own for this long.

"Hmm," I mumbled, looking at the notifications.

"Is everything OK?" Uncle Jack stood and approached me.

I shrugged. "I'm not sure."

He retrieved my phone and looked at the message. "What does this mean?"

My head throbbed. What would this do to the bakery? I had been riding a high for quite some time with the popularity and growth. Naively, it never occurred to me that people wouldn't like it, let alone post scathing reviews.

Taking my phone back, I silenced it as several more notifications appeared with essentially the same message.

"I set up an alert on-line to be notified if the bakery got critical reviews." I put my hand on my forehead to stall the pain. Would people believe what was being written? Was the bakery in trouble? What could I do to counteract the unfair barrage?

"Who wrote that? Let me see," Uncle Jack bellowed, his papa bear emerging.

"I forgot the alert was even there. I've gotten nothing below a three star the entire time I've been open." Tears formed in my eyes. The reviews weren't even about the food.

"Can you do anything about this?" Unkie asked Barney.

"It's pretty tough to discover who's doing that. But unless it's harassment or something illegal, we likely wouldn't get involved."

"Is it?" Uncle Jack asked me.

I inhaled to stave off the tears. I needed to develop a thicker skin for this business stuff. "No. Just a lot of comments about us shutting down the booth at the tournament without letting anyone buy anything." I stuttered a breath. "Some aren't even reviews, just a one star rating."

"When can you clear the tournament to start up again?" Uncle Jack probed Barney for answers. That by itself wouldn't erase the bad reviews. But how could I negate them with more positives?

Barney pursed his lips. The investigation would take the time it took. With so many people to interview, it wouldn't be done any time soon unless they got a lucky break.

Uncle Jack continued, "Spill it." He could pressure his friend like I couldn't.

Joining Unkie in the inquisition, I said, "Barney?" He had done well keeping a neutral demeanor, but something percolated underneath that veneer.

"I really can't say much right now," he said. "We still have a lot more investigation to do."

My gut told me where this was going. Dexter remained at the forefront of suspects.

"Barney, no," I pleaded. "It can't be. I'm positive."

"I know what you're saying, Tilly. And I don't want to believe it either. But there are incriminations that I can't yet explain away."

What was he intimating? What evidence did he have against Dexter?

"Sometimes things aren't as they appear," I said, completely convinced Dexter didn't kill Caden. But was he involved in some way? Did he know something he was covering up? Was he taking the brunt for a friend?

"I agree. But our computer forensics team has come across some on-line chats that are pretty damning."

My heart sank. Explaining away trash talk might be hard to do. Did the competition get so fierce that someone took it off-line and made it personal?

"Are you going to arrest him?" We referred to Dexter without mentioning his name. I stood, head up, and shoulders back. By the time I returned to the bakery, I had to paste on a stoic face. I couldn't let on to Dexter what might be coming.

Barney stayed silent. I had little time before this evolved to the inevitable. The bakery reviews took a backseat to uncovering the real killer and exonerating Dexter. I sped to the door without a word.

"Tilly?" Barney said.

With my hand on the doorknob, I paused without turning around. "I know." And Barney knew too. I couldn't help but do my thing to find out what really happened in that practice room at the tournament. Dexter had a key to the puzzle, whether he realized it or not. I wouldn't go against Barney's wishes, but that didn't mean I wouldn't bend the rules.

Leaving Unkie's shop, my heart was heavy, and my stomach churned, and not because of the fruitcake. I only had a short amount of time to get myself together and figure out how I would have the conversation with Dexter without letting on about the impending conclusion of the investigation. I refused to let my mind go to the place where Dexter caused a death.

The on-line chats Barney referred to were public. How could I get to those to find out what they had said? I knew the game was called Gridiron Gash. Could I create an account there myself to see what they had posted? For the first time, I felt encouraged that I had an action plan. If I could see the conversation, I could better guide my questions to Dexter.

I bounded into the bakery and stopped in my tracks. Typically, the lobby and the booths were packed at this time of the morning. Nobody was here. I checked the sign on the door to confirm the Open part was facing outward. Peeking outside, I looked for anyone that might be making their way here. Bupkis. I pushed that issue to the side and headed back to the kitchen.

Noah and Dexter were having a loud conversation that must have prevented them from hearing the bell on the door when I arrived. I grabbed an apron, anticipating and willing customers to arrive. The display case remained full from the first baking of the day. If we didn't get people soon, a whole lot of pastries would go to waste.

"I'm telling you, we killed their team," Dexter said.

I stepped closer to the kitchen door. Were they talking about the video game?

"Caden didn't deserve to win," Dexter continued. "Gavin's pretty sure he knows how he cheated."

That kid wasn't helping his case. I really needed to counsel him about his words while the investigation was happening.

"Well, hopefully you'll get a chance once the tournament starts up again," Noah said.

"Yeah, with Caden gone, I think I could really win this year," Dexter said.

CHAPTER SEVEN

I was getting a second chance to make a first impression. Justin and his parents were meeting me for dinner at Tuscany's, a somewhat upscale Italian restaurant. I had left home with double the time I actually needed to travel to the restaurant and still be early. However, I must have been in a time warp, losing minutes of my life. Glancing at my phone, I saw digits confirming I would be late. How could that happen?

The temperature of the day had cooled as the sun dipped into the ocean, but my face glistened with sweat. I huffed it even faster in my heels to minimize my tardiness, hoping I didn't splat right there on the sidewalk. I wore heels about once a year, always opting for more comfy sneakers since I had to be on my feet all day.

Entering the restaurant, I approached the hostess stand, and she pointed me to a corner with a view of the beach. Hopefully, that ambiance had softened the blow of my being late. All three pivoted toward me as I approached.

Justin popped up and guided me into my chair and whispered, "Relax."

Avoiding an apology for being late and drawing attention to it, I said, "It's a beautiful evening."

Patricia looked at her watch and then toward Albert. He shook his head.

"Yes, it is," Justin replied. "Maybe we should have gotten a table outside." The outdoor seating was under lights strung all around the patio and had portable propane heaters. Sometimes it was warmer out there than inside.

Patricia silently picked up her menu and stared at it.

"If you like ravioli, they have an excellent spinach pesto version. And they make all of their pasta from scratch," I said. How could I get the conversation going to be more collegial?

Patrick pointed to something on Patricia's menu, and she nodded.

I sat back in my seat and glanced at Justin. He shrugged.

"We stopped by Jack's yesterday," Justin said. It might just be up to him to lead the way to carry this conversation.

Turning to Patricia and Albert, I said, "He mentioned that. What did you think?"

I waited for what seemed like minutes, but in reality it was probably two seconds. "He's delightful. And that place was lots of fun," Patricia said. She set her menu on the table and placed a hand on it. "I saw a few things I'd like to go back for." She grinned at Albert.

"Yes, dear," he said. I chuckled. Smart man.

"He gushed over you," Patricia said, her face returning to a stoic expression.

The server interrupted to take our order. I hoped they hurried with the food. This felt like an inquisition that I might never escape.

"Tilly's come a long way in the short time she's been in Belle Harbor," Justin offered.

Yes, I had. I thought that counted for something. But his parents' veneer wasn't cracking. What was it about me that wasn't clicking?

"He told us you left Boston. Why would you come all the way out here?" Albert asked, joining the fray.

Maybe I was thinking about this all wrong. What if their questioning wasn't because they didn't like me? What if that was just their way to get to know me? Though their expressions belied their motives. I always asked a lot of questions, especially when I was sleuthing. Did I come across in the same way that they were? I settled into my seat and decided I needed to be myself. If they didn't like me, that was on them.

With my hands in my lap, I crossed my fingers tightly on both hands under the table. Here went nothing. "Originally, I came for my Uncle Frank's memorial service."

They both nodded.

OK, it was now or never. I felt Justin drape his arm along the back of my chair and place his hand lightly on my back. "Honestly, I needed a change. My husband cheated on me. Unkie, er, Uncle Jack offered for me to stay with him to get back on my feet." There, it was out like a flounder flopping in the middle of the table.

"Hmph," Patricia made a noise. What did that mean? Justin knew all about my history and loved me anyway. If my life circumstances turned off his parents, there wasn't anything I could do. I didn't choose it.

"Well, before we leave town, we'll come see your bakery," Albert said. Wow, had my truthfulness broken the ice?

"That would be lovely," I said. "It's named after my grandma Luna, who had her own place."

Justin squeezed my shoulder for encouragement. "Tilly does really well."

"I would love to treat you to our signature cream-filled cupcake, her favorite recipe," I said.

"Oh no," Patricia said, waving her hand at the idea.

So close. Maybe I should adjust my expectations. One visit with Justin's parents wouldn't make us best friends. I so wanted this to work. Maybe a visit to their home in Arizona, on their turf. Relationships take time; I soothed myself with that thought.

The server brought our steaming plates of pasta. I couldn't wait to dig in for some comfort.

Patricia looked at her watch again. *Dang, lady.* It seemed she was eager to be done with me.

Albert reached into his pocket and retrieved a pill box, handing it to Patricia. She glanced at her watch again. Was she tracking the time for her medication? Had I completely misread the signals this entire time? And it wasn't about my being late at all?

"Mom is lactose intolerant," Justin leaned in, saying this in a loud whisper.

Of course, so my offer of cupcakes was inappropriate. Got it. "We have quite a variety of pastries. I hope you'll find something you like."

"I'm sure we will," Albert said. "We both have quite the sweet tooth."

My brain exploded. Every single one of their responses I interpreted as them not liking me, when there was a completely logical explanation. Why didn't I use my sleuthing technique, allowing the evidence to lead to the right conclusion? My desire for them to like me the minute they met me caused me to behave outside the norm.

"I like that little blue streak in your hair," Patricia said.

This night had turned a one-eighty from where it started. I was prepared to leave dinner with the conclusion they didn't approve of me for their son. Reaching my hand to my head, I said, "Thank you."

Justin grabbed for my hand under the table and squeezed. With this turn of events, I might now be able to concentrate on Dexter. That kid was digging himself further into a hole. I wouldn't interfere to the degree that it would influence Barney's investigation, but that boy needed some guidance. Somebody at that tournament had killed Caden. Dexter knew a lot of people there. Without upsetting him, I needed to grill him for details. He may just have the clue to this whole thing without realizing it.

CHAPTER EIGHT

I was still flying on cloud nine from the dinner with Justin and his parents. There was enough movement in a positive direction that I had hope. Unkie's instincts about people were always spot on. I should have trusted him. Early at the bakery, I had arrived before anyone else, buzzing around the kitchen in preparation for the second baking of the day, hopeful we would have more customers today.

Wracking my brain for what to do to deal with the negative reviews, I about jumped through the ceiling when Dexter arrived through the back door.

"What happened in here?" he asked.

I glanced around. Empty mixing bowls, trays and dishes abounded, along with a light coating of flour everywhere. Without him picking up behind me, they had piled up. Shrugging, I said, "I couldn't sleep."

Maybe keeping him busy while we talked about Caden was an excellent strategy to minimize him getting upset. He grabbed his apron and began loading dishes into the dishwasher and sink.

Dexter pivoted and leaned up against the sink, crossing his arms. He gazed around the kitchen. "Do you think we're going to get any more customers today?" His cheeks were drawn.

I pulled my hands out of the dough and approached him. "This has nothing to do with you."

He dropped his head and scuffed his foot forward. "I know, but-"

"Dexter, look at me." That boy was putting everything on his shoulders. He likely felt that way as the oldest child at home with a single mom.

"Tilly." Tears emerged. I had never seen any emotion but youthful exuberance from him. My heart clenched.

I took him by the hand to a couple of chairs along the back wall. "Dexter, it'll be OK. Trust me." I had to convince him, even if I had my own doubts.

He sniffled. "I don't know."

"Well, I do." Inhaling, I decided it was now or never. "Dexter, I heard you saying some things about Caden the other day."

Turning to face me, more tears poured out. His bottom lip quivered. "I didn't like him very much." He dropped his head.

"I get that. But until they catch the killer, I think you need to be careful what you say." Was that enough for him to get the message?

"He didn't deserve to win last year. Gavin knows exactly how he cheated." He sat tall.

"Be that as it may, it doesn't sound good when you say that."

The front doorbell jingled. Glancing at the wall clock, I saw we were past the time to open. That sound buoyed my hopes for a better day. We both stood.

"I understand, Tilly." He grinned, the demeanor of our lovable guy returning. "Um, would you like me to go wait on the customer?" He looked me up and down.

"Yes, go." I chuckled, watching him lope through the swinging door. Had I gotten through to him? If he could just hold his tongue a little longer, the police could progress on their investigation. But would he? When he got together with his friends, I suspected all bets were off. I did the best I could.

Laughter came from the front of the café. The female voice was familiar. Both she and Dexter were now guffawing. Oh, the best medicine for that boy. He poked his head through the door and said, "Tilly, come see who's here." I didn't much care if they were going to spend money.

I looked down at myself, dried dough on my apron, and icing smears to top it off. Well, this was a bakery.

Hoping to see a lobby full of people, I slowed my pace at seeing one person. But that was a start.

"Hello, dear," Maude said.

The elderly woman visiting with her friend Mabel had helped take down a thief and murderer. Surprised to see she was still here, I said, "Hi, Maude. You're still in town."

She stepped to my side, giving my arm a slight squeeze. "Yes, Mabel had to get back to her Treehouse Hotel. But I love this place so much, I had to stay a bit longer."

"I'm glad you did." I pointed to the pastry case. "Dexter, can you get Maude anything she wants?"

"Oh no, hon. I'm here to buy everything you have."

I stepped back, uncertain I clearly heard what she said.

She laughed. "I saw what those trolls on-line did to your reviews."

This woman was up on technology. She was a former cyber-security analyst. My head exploded with the possibility she might be able to check out the on-line chat that Barney had mentioned.

"I'm here to do business, and I'm going to donate all of it to the first responders."

Dexter was already behind the counter, loading everything into boxes. I was stunned. "That's so generous of you."

"And I'm going to take care of those trolls." I had no idea what she meant by that. How could you make something on the Internet go away? I assumed she meant virtually and not in reality. That's all I needed, another crime on my hands.

"Maude, I don't know what to say." I wrapped her up in a sticky, floury hug. "Oh, I'm so sorry." I brushed off the crumbs I had left on her shoulder.

She threw her head back. "I'll take that any day." If only she would stay in town. I would love to get to know her better. She was a hoot. I needed more of that in my life. Holding her hand to the side of her mouth, she leaned in and loudly whispered, "I have a secret I wanted to share with Dexter."

A thud came from behind the counter. Dexter looked up, red-faced. "I'm so sorry, Tilly." A box of cupcakes had hit the floor. I scurried behind the counter to help him.

Maude continued with her mysterious comments. "I know you're a gamer," she said to Dexter.

He looked at me as if to ask permission to respond. I was grateful he had retained some of our earlier discussion. "Yes. I was supposed to play at the tournament this weekend. But-" He thoughtfully halted.

"Me too," Maude replied.

I continued filling the remaining boxes with all the pastries. If more customers arrived, we would have to do some double time baking.

"Oh, is your grandson playing?" Dexter asked.

"No. I am," Maude said.

How could that be? You had to qualify through local tournaments to get to this big one. Was there even more to this granny than met the eye? She was slow-walking Dexter somewhere as she smirked.

"But, how?" Dexter said.

"Have you heard of slaya65?" Maude asked, pointing to herself.

"No way!" he yelled. "You're a legend."

Turning toward me, he said, "Tilly, do you know who that is?"

"I've heard you talk about that player before. Maude, is that really you?" I asked, just as bewildered as Dexter at the revelation.

"In the flesh. And Dexter, I have an offer for you."

Dexter and his friends had always assumed that the player was a teenage boy. Maude had just flipped the script. They wouldn't believe it.

"While we're waiting for the tournament to start back up, I'd be happy to tutor you so that you're ready when it does."

Another box of pastries hit the floor.

CHAPTER NINE

I questioned my sanity as my small cottage living room filled with teenage boys. I had agreed to host Maude's mentoring session with Dexter and his friends. Knowing they would eat me out of house and home, I had stopped and filled several bags from Tuscany, hoping pasta would do the trick to fill them up.

Maude had arrived with a giant box of gear, which she described as game consoles and controllers. Cables and cords were draped everywhere. My little Peanut peeked out of the bedroom door. It was normally just the two of us. Her eyes were now as big as saucers with the growing volume of voices. I chuckled. Both of us would sleep well tonight.

Joining me in the kitchen to prep the food, Maude said, "This was very generous of you, Tilly."

"The generosity is all you. Even if Dexter doesn't win the tournament, you've just made his dream come true." This would at least distract him for a bit from the reality of Caden's murder. And give me a chance to observe and see the interaction that might give me a clue.

"Tilly, you should join us," Dexter yelled from the other room.

"Uh, no. This is all you, kiddo," I said.

"Your loss. You might really enjoy it," Dexter said.

I couldn't see how. And just observing the chaos in my cottage was entertainment enough. The boys swarmed the kitchen for their plates, practically inhaling the food. I gazed around at what I thought was going to be days of leftovers. At this rate, the boys would devour everything by the end of the night.

"Alright, boys. Gather around," Maude ordered. She sat in a center chair like she was on a throne with her subjects surrounding her. All eyes were on the expert as she held court for the now silent audience. They all held a controller in their hands as she leaned forward and pressed the power button on the console. The game roared to life on my little TV in the corner.

I pulled out a chair from the eating bar and settled in for the show.

"Do you have the cheat codes or something?" Gavin asked.

Maude whipped her head in his direction and glared.

"What?" Gavin looked around to garner support from his friends for the comment. "I mean…" he gestured toward Maude, saying what everyone was likely thinking. How could this unassuming granny be a hotshot video game player? It defied conventional logic, but wasn't impossible. I had the question myself and couldn't wait to see how she took these boys to school.

"OK, Gavin. You're first up," Maude said.

His eyes widened, and his shoulders slumped.

Maude signed into the game with her name, slaya65. I was certain I heard a gasp from the boys. To be in the flesh with a legend of the game. Gavin signed in and they prepared to start the game.

Maude sat back and said, "Now, before we start, a couple of pointers." She regaled the group with her sage advice about how to navigate the football moves. She sounded like a coach who had played the game for decades. I doubted Maude had ever set foot on the gridiron. How in the world would she know so much without playing the game?

"But if I don't dog the running back, he's going to end run," Gavin said.

Softly, Maude patiently replied with her logic for the specific move she advised. All the boys nodded in unison. This scene was as entertaining as any comedy club event I had ever attended.

The kickoff ensued, and Gavin ran the ball all the way back for a touchdown, expertly dodging Maude's players during the entire sprint. Uh oh. What was happening? The boys cheered.

Non-plussed, Maude received the kickoff to her player and expertly navigated several yards up the field to a chorus of groans. Now I wondered if she was toying with Gavin. She paused the game and pointed at the screen. "Is that your comment?" A chat window appeared to the right of the main playing field. It accused Caden of cheating and proceeded to incriminate Gavin with comments about taking Caden out.

Quickly scanning the room, Gavin pleaded, "It's just trash talk. Everyone does it." He stood. "I had nothing to do with Caden. You have to believe me."

I supposed most things taken out of context could make the person look guilty. That on-line chat was going to be a challenge to sort through and tease out any real clues. Gavin's shoulders dropped. He wouldn't be alone with incriminating comments. Dexter stood and patted his friend's shoulder. This mystery was taking its toll on these boys.

Maude resumed the game and said, "Let's get back to it. I have a lot more to show you." No doubt. She looked at me and winked. I was eternally grateful for her generosity to not only tutor these boys, but provide them a distraction. This would be a memory they would talk about for quite some time. Maude and Gavin continued their game, Gavin gaining a small advantage right before Maude completely took over. I suspected she was going easy on him, not wanting to totally embarrass the kid.

"Dang, you're good," Dexter said.

"You're the next victim." Gavin sat back against the couch and handed the controller to Dexter.

"I thought I might have a chance to win this year. But Maude, you've probably got this in the bag," Dexter said.

"You can do it, Dexter," Gavin encouraged. He high-fived Wayne who had silently sat back watching the show.

"Yeah, that record prize. Wish I was good enough to have a chance at it," Wayne said. "Just glad Caden won't be getting it."

All heads pivoted toward Wayne. He held his hands up. "Whoa. You know he cheated. We just don't know exactly how."

"I'm telling you, it was an inside job," Gavin said.

Maude leaned forward and reset the game to start another round. "What do you mean?" Ah, excellent open-ended question. My ears perked up.

"This is going to sound bad," Gavin started. "Caden just wasn't that smart or good to make it all the way to the end of the tournament."

"Gav," Dexter said, fidgeting in his seat.

"You know it's true. You're so much better and deserve it way more," Gavin said.

"Do you mean there was another player that took the fall so Caden could win?" Maude said.

That was quite the accusation. Who could that be? If we knew that, we might be a lot further in this investigation. Would that person have turned on Caden for some reason?

"We'll never know, now that Caden is dead," Wayne said.

Maude snuck a peek at me over her shoulder. I nodded.

"I might have a way to find out," Maude said. That woman had her means to sleuth out things on-line I was afraid to know were possible.

"How?" Dexter asked.

"I have my ways. Don't you worry about that."

He grinned. It warmed my heart to see him enjoying himself, even if he was about to get creamed in the game he loved.

CHAPTER TEN

I had seen the professionally designed posters and flyers for Florence's Tasty Cakes everywhere. They all said the same thing: "Taste the divine deliciousness of Florence's Tasty Cakes!" My jaw clenched as I read the bold text, the bright colors of the advertisement. She was obviously taking this to the next level. I had to do something about it.

The flyer even listed a social media account for the cakes. The designs on the flyer looked very similar to what an art student had designed for Uncle Jack. During the arts walk earlier this year, Taylor had displayed her work at Unkie's antique shop.

With my heart pounding in my chest, I peeked from the bakery window where Florence had cakes stacked high. Not one customer had come to the bakery this morning, but Florence had a long line of people waiting to buy from her. Was it all because of the marketing that her customer base had quickly grown? I made a note to get in touch with Taylor to hire her for the bakery. It certainly couldn't hurt to counteract those bad reviews we had received.

Leaving the bakery, I set off for the beachside cake stand. It seemed as if every step I took was a reminder of the competition I was about to face. I was determined to confront Florence and let her know I wasn't about to let her take my business away without a fight. While it wasn't her fault I got the scathing ratings, she wasn't helping the situation.

I took a deep breath and marched up to the stand. "Hi, Florence," I said, gripping my hands for courage.

Florence smiled brightly. "It's nice to see you, Tilly. What can I get you?" She pulled out a paper plate and swept her arm along the table. I had to admit, those little fruitcakes looked amazing, even better than the other day. I knew first hand they tasted excellent. Maybe the bright sun shining put them in a new light.

"Do you have passion fruit?" A customer asked.

"Oh, dear. That would be a delightful flavor. Not yet, but come back next time," Florence said.

I felt a twinge of envy as I scanned the table and the lovingly displayed cakes that were being bought by droves of customers. My stomach dropped as I turned to see the empty bakery window. It seemed like no matter what I did, I couldn't bring the customers back. I had to think out of the box.

Florence was giddy as she continued to hand out the cakes. The pineapple scent from the table wafted my way, causing my mouth to water.

Standing to Florence's side, I ventured forward with my brainstormed idea. "What would you think about a collaboration?" Using Florence's cakes, maybe I could draw customers back to the bakery.

"What do you mean?" she asked, wiping her hands on her apron and turning toward me.

I shaded my eyes from the sun, looking her straight in the eye. "Well, how about we feature your cakes at the bakery?"

Shaking her head, she just said, "No."

My shoulders slumped. OK. That was just the first answer. Maybe going to her passion was the answer. "If you allow us to make the cakes at the bakery, you can spend more time at your store."

"I just don't know." Florence continued to serve customers. She was enjoying this. Maybe it wasn't meant to be. Would the partnership be more trouble than it was worth?

"You would have full creative control," I offered. What would I have to concede to seal the deal? There wasn't much I wouldn't do to make this happen. It could really get the bakery in the black again. Even one day without customers was a tremendous hit to the bottom line.

"You're on the right track," she said, handing a bag to a customer with a dozen cakes in it. By my calculation, she had done several hundred dollars of business in just the few minutes since I had arrived. Oh, what I wouldn't give to have that flowing into my cash register.

"You could train us on the recipe to your satisfaction," I continued on.

Florence gasped, slapping a hand over her mouth. "Oh, I completely forgot that."

What did I miss? Our path to a deal just took a detour.

She shook her head. I waited for a clue to my next step. "You'd need to sign a non-disclosure agreement for the recipe," she said.

"Of course." My skin prickled at the prospect that we had a deal in principle. This might just be what turned the bakery around. Florence had created excitement and high demand for her cakes, to the degree customers were requesting new flavors. "Thank you, Florence."

Our relationship had been rocky up to this point. I hoped this new business venture would smooth that out.

"Two of my favorite ladies," came a booming voice from behind us, causing me to jump. "Whoa. Sorry about that, Tilly." Barney placed a hand on my back. "Do I need to get my apron out again?" He peered over the table, now sparsely showing just a few cakes remaining.

Glancing at Florence, I waited for her to respond with the news.

"I think you're off the hook," she said.

I exhaled with gratitude.

Barney looked at me with furrowed brows. "No more baking?"

Florence grinned. "Tilly and I have forged a new partnership."

With relief, I gave Florence a side hug. "You can still come help at the bakery if you want to keep your hands in the dough." I chuckled.

"Speaking of dough," Barney said.

I didn't think this was a coincidental, friendly visit. A pit formed in my gut, certain of where he was headed with the line of questioning. I snuck a peek at the deserted bakery where Dexter was inside with Noah, continuing to bake. In the off chance we got customers, I couldn't not be ready. Even if we had to donate uneaten pastries again, I didn't want to risk turning away any customer because we were out of products.

Placing a hand on my stomach, I said, "Let's go." Maybe if I broke the news to Dexter, it might ease the blow. Barney's follow-up questions to Dexter meant there was more to uncover and possibly incriminate him.

"I'm really sorry, Tilly," Barney said as he gave Florence a departing kiss on the cheek. "You as well as anyone know that I have to follow the evidence where it leads me."

What could I say to that? No way Dexter killed Caden. But did he know something? Was he covering for a friend? Did they plan something together that got out of hand? I shuffled my feet, attempting to delay the inevitable. Barney kept my snail's pace. I wracked my brain for the words to use with Dexter when we reached the bakery. Barney held the door as I entered the echo chamber with a quick glimpse at Florence's stand. At least one part of my life was looking up.

We entered the empty lobby to the sound of pans clanging from the kitchen.

Dexter bounded through the swinging door and halted as he spotted Barney.

CHAPTER ELEVEN

ehind us, Maude entered the bakery's empty lobby. My head was so consumed by the impending conversation, I hadn't even noticed her behind us.

"Is everything OK?" Maude pointed her question at Barney.

Barney's gaze was distant. "I have more questions about some evidence," he replied with a vague response. What was it that prompted a follow-up visit?

At the mention of evidence, Dexter's eyes raised in an arc. "What evidence? What's going on?" he asked.

Barney's face softened as he spoke. "There's been some on-line chat that incriminates you," he said.

Without another word, Dexter silently left the room to get his backpack. Maude didn't move, her eyes locked on Barney as he watched Dexter leave.

When he was gone, Maude finally spoke. "Tilly, it's serious, but Dexter didn't do anything wrong," she said. She held up her phone to show me the on-line chat.

It was full of alarming words, threats that could only mean something bad. Maude's voice was soft, a whisper of comfort. "He's going to be alright," she said.

I took a deep breath and nodded.

Dexter returned to the room, his face pasted with worry. Maude held out her phone to him, showing him the chat. He scanned it quickly before looking back up at Barney.

"What does this mean?" Dexter asked, his voice carrying a hint of desperation.

Barney sighed heavily, his eyes darting between the three of them. "I don't know yet," he admitted. "But I need to take you down to the station for questioning."

Dexter's face paled, and he took a step back. "I didn't do anything wrong," he protested.

"I know, son," Barney said gently. "But we need to get to the bottom of this. And until we do, you're going to have to come with me."

I stepped forward, placing a reassuring hand on Dexter's shoulder. "We'll be right there with you," I said firmly, with no underlying confidence. My heart raced. Was Barney downplaying the evidence so that he didn't upset Dexter?

Dexter and Barney exited the bakery, the door closing with a heavy thud. The air in the room thickened with worry. Until this was resolved, I wasn't convinced Dexter wouldn't take the fall for the murder.

I plopped into a booth and laid my head on my hands. Maude slid in to the opposite seat, reaching to squeeze my hand. Lifting my head, my voice quivered. "He's innocent."

She nodded.

"Can I see your phone again?" I asked.

Maude punched in her screen code to unlock it and slid it across the table.

Oh boy. How would Dexter ever explain that? The text said *I'm going to make Caden regret ever challenging me.*

"Maude, you've played this game for a long time. Is that normal chatter?" I asked.

She retrieved her phone and scrolled, returning it to me. I squeezed my eyes closed. This was getting worse. *I'm going to show Caden what happens when you mess with the wrong person.*

"It is," she replied. "But it's never preceded someone's death."

I sat back in the booth, the faux leather seat squeaking loudly in the empty room. "There's got to be more to this."

"I agree." She halted.

"Maude?" I leaned forward. "What is it?" It couldn't get worse, could it?

She had sources that might just outperform Barney's detectives in sleuthing out on-line activity.

"I know it looks bad," I said. "But just because someone has a motive, doesn't mean that prompted them to do anything about it. That kid has a huge heart." The money and prizes from the competition would literally be life-changing, not just for Dexter, but also his family.

"I don't want to say too much until Barney has a chance to look into it." Maude evaded sharing any details.

"Can you give me a hint?" I asked, desperate for any nugget of encouragement.

Maude looked around and lowered her voice. That gesture must have been instinct, as there was nobody else in the lobby.

"The tournament finances were in the toilet. If they had to pay out, it would cause them to go under," she said.

That revelation opened up a whole new set of suspects. But why kill Caden?

I leaned forward, my mind racing with new possibilities. "Do you think someone at the tournament is behind this?" I asked.

Maude nodded. "I'm not sure who yet, but it's possible. I heard rumors of embezzlement and financial trouble before the tournament even started."

My heart sank. "So you think they might have killed Caden to cover up their financial troubles?"

"It's a possibility," Maude said cautiously, as if she didn't want to jump to conclusions.

We sat in silence for a few moments, both lost in thought. I couldn't shake the feeling that we were missing something important.

Maude leaned in further, almost as if she was afraid someone might overhear. "I heard rumors that Caden had a side deal going on with the judges, rigging the competition in favor of certain players," she whispered.

My eyes widened. "That's a huge accusation," I said.

Maude's eyebrows knitted together as she spoke. "It's possible that Caden found out about the financial troubles and threatened to go public. It's also possible that he was killed for a completely different reason altogether, and the cheating was just a red herring."

I nodded, taking in everything she said. "Do you think Dexter could be in danger?" I asked, worried.

Maude shook her head. "I don't think so," she said. "But we need to find out who's behind all of this before anyone else gets hurt."

Before I could even formulate a plan, the door to the bakery swung open, and Barney and Dexter walked back in. Barney looked tense, and Dexter looked like he was about to be sick.

"That was fast. What happened?" I asked, standing up from the booth.

Barney sighed heavily.

"We have some leads, but it's going to take some time to sort everything out," he said, looking at each of us. "For now, I'm going to take Dexter home. He's not a suspect, but I need to make sure he's safe."

I felt a temporary sense of relief wash over me.

Dexter turned to face me. "I'm sorry, Tilly. I didn't mean for any of this to happen," he said.

I reached out and took his hand, giving it a reassuring squeeze. "We'll figure this out."

As they left the bakery, Maude turned to me with a determined look on her face. "We need to find out who's really behind this," she said firmly.

I nodded in agreement. "Let's start by looking into the financial troubles of the tournament and see if we can find any links to Caden's murder," I said.

Maude pulled out her phone and started typing furiously. "I'll start digging through my sources and see if I can find any information about the judges and their potential involvement in the rigging," she said.

My heart raced, feeling closer to solving this than ever before. *Hang in there, Dexter.* I wondered if they would allow him back into the tournament, or if it would continue. But I needed to make it OK for that kid.

CHAPTER TWELVE

"Did you find anything?"

Maude pounded her phone keyboard faster than I could. At that speed, my auto correct would be working double time. And who knows what gobbledygook would come out the other side?

"Maybe."

I stood and moved to the light switch in the lobby. The sun was setting, and the room darkening. Our time to exonerate Dexter and find the killer was dwindling. From watching crime shows, I knew that the first 48 hours were the most critical to solving a murder.

"I've been investigating the other players in the tournament," Maude said. "I'm wondering if someone knew about the financial troubles and had a motive to kill Caden."

My phone buzzed. I looked up at Maude. "What is this?"

"I sent you some chat logs. If you could help scan through, it'll go faster," she said.

The text on my screen looked like another language. "OK. What am I looking for?"

"Honestly, hon. You'll know it when you see it. Trust me."

My eyes burned from squinting at the small text, attempting to locate any nuggets that might be helpful. I gasped.

Not only were others trash talking, there were more statements by Dexter about doing Caden in. I turned my phone over and placed it on the table, unable to go on. Maybe it was better I not know.

Heading to the window, I gazed at the sun dipping into the ocean, the stars beginning to appear in the twilight. To my right, Florence and Taylor were closing up her stand. I had put my hope in Florence's hands to get the bakery up and running again. Would I even be able to recover from the lost business?

"Tilly? Let's take a break. I know this can be emotionally exhausting."

I slipped back into the booth, gazing around the lobby. My mom had helped with the interior design of the bakery. The blue and white color combination, the style of tables and chairs, the serving ware. Oh, it would devastate her if the bakery had to shut down. I couldn't go there.

"Dexter is the most important thing right now," I said, interlacing my fingers and squeezing tight.

"But there's more." That woman had an eye for things off-kilter. We were so lucky she had agreed to stay in Belle Harbor a few more days. I don't know what I would have done without her investigative skills and resources. With my mind elsewhere, Dexter might have been in serious trouble.

"Yeah." I glanced around. "Not just the bakery, but-" Was I being overly dramatic? I had done my best at the two meetings with Justin's parents. That's all I could ask of myself.

Maude reached across the table and gripped my hand.

I sniffled. "It's just that-" I couldn't get the words out. A heaviness settled into my chest. Everything accumulating was too much. I burst into tears.

She got up and scooted next to me on the seat, draping her arm around my shoulders. I leaned my head on her, shuddering a few sobs. She patiently held me. I felt like I had used every ounce of energy I had remaining.

Slowly, I started. "Justin's parents are leaving soon and I don't think they like me." How junior high did that sound? But those were my legitimate feelings.

Maude returned to the other side of the booth. "Do you want me to investigate them?" she said with all seriousness.

Laughing, I said, "No. But thanks." I didn't want to know anything she might find out. "I think I just need to give it time."

"That sounds wise," she said.

I would meet up with Justin and his parents one last time before they left. My goal was to be my completely authentic self. And then let any remaining expectations go.

"Thank you, Maude."

She stood and paced in a circle around the lobby, her pointer finger tapping on her chin. No telling where her mind was now.

"I'm just wondering," she started as she headed toward the wall, gently touching my grandmother's photo.

My heart galloped. No way I would go down without a fight for this bakery in my grandmother's name. No way.

Maude turned. "I see a lot of her in you." She returned to the booth. "And I venture a guess she would have a bevy of ideas for how to save the bakery."

"I think you two would have been besties," I said. And no doubt the terrors of the town.

A whoosh of air blasted into the lobby as the bakery door opened. A customer? Even at this late hour? I bounded up, ready to treat them like royalty. My heart dropped as I saw Florence peek her head in the door.

"Can we come in?" she asked, looking behind her.

"Of course." Who asks permission to come into a business?

She waved her arm and entered the room.

"I brought some friends with me," she said as about a dozen women trailed her, most about Florence's age.

I looked at Maude. She shrugged, neither of us having a clue as to what was happening.

"I know they unfairly targeted you on-line for reviews and we're here to help," Florence said.

"OK." What in the world did they have in mind? I looked at the women, some who smiled, others who had their game faces on. If Florence was determined for something to happen, I was confident she would get her way.

Stepping forward, Florence said, "These are some of my book club ladies."

That explained nothing. It felt like she was slow-walking me to a conclusion, and I had no energy to finish the race. I waited.

"We're going to buy your pastries and then post reviews about them," she said.

"Are you serious?" I said, just a little quieter than a shout. I approached Florence with my arms wide to give her a giant hug. Was this woman who gave me a hard time softening even further toward me?

"What's happened to you isn't right," she said. "We've got lots of friends and family in this town. So you better get to baking up a storm." Florence approached Maude, pulling a phone out of her apron pocket. "And can you show me how to work this thing so we can leave reviews?"

"Oh, Florence," I said. If the bakery business turned around, that would be one less thing on my mind so that I could focus solely on making sure Dexter was OK. "You have no idea what this means."

"We help each other in this town, darlin.'" She strutted around the room, clearly loving the role of being in charge. I would have to wrack my brain to see how she might play a larger role in the bakery. She had connections with high-level people in the town. And her and my budding relationship might mean incredible possibilities for the business. "I know how hard you've worked for this place." She walked toward my grandmother's picture. "Family is everything."

That woman melted my heart. From where we started when we first met, we had come a long way. I needed to apply that same patience and perseverance to Justin's parents.

CHAPTER THIRTEEN

My heart was torn into pieces. While Barney had agreed to let the tournament go on, Dexter was not out of the woods yet as a suspect in Caden's death.

I stood in the back of the mammoth conference center main stage, surveying the players to figure out which of them might be involved.

Dexter and his friends huddled in a section to my right. Maude's tutoring of them had raised their confidence through the roof. But if Dexter won, would there even be prize money to pay out? After all of that work, would he be rewarded with a win?

Maude had uncovered fraud in the tournament, but it wasn't clear whether the sponsoring company knew of it.

The main screen in the center of the room roared to life with animated football players flexing their muscles. By my calculation, Dexter had to win seven rounds in order to be in the final two. If he lost at any point, that number of games doubled in order to get out of the loser's bracket.

With play starting, the food court was a ghost-town. All the players had loaded up trays of snacks to settle in for the next round.

"Hello, Tilly."

I jumped several inches, slapping my hand over my chest. "Florence." I gazed around. "What are you doing here?"

Florence had baked several batches of her cakes and delivered them to me first thing this morning.

"This is kind of exciting," she said, without a clue of the underlying drama.

Our budding business partnership gave me hope my bakery would jumpstart me back to success.

"It is, isn't it?"

Maude had taken a place in the center of the front row, her status in the game catapulting her to royalty. The teen boys in here remained skeptical of her gaming prowess. They were about to be schooled. That possibility was more exciting to me than watching the screen. Little did they know she had an ulterior motive.

Maude and Barney had devised a plan where her cyber buddies would be on-line in chat. Apparently, they had some kind of on-line tools that could alert them under certain conditions. The whole thing blew my mind when Maude described to me what they could do. One of Maude's proteges in the cyber community, named Stephanie, was an expert at data analytics. She could see patterns that could, in turn, make predictions.

Slaya65 flashed across the big screen as the first game was about to begin. As Maude did her thing, how would we know if something was happening?

Florence had brought a tray of cakes with her and was making her way up and down the aisles, delivering them to the players. After a quick double-take at the fruitcakes, the kids devoured them.

I took a seat in the back row, along the aisle. Wiping my sweaty hands on my apron, I glanced at Dexter. He and his friends had their heads together, pointing at a smaller screen on the left. How could anyone keep track of what was happening with multiple games playing simultaneously?

I saw motion from my right side, Kenneth making his way toward me. Smiling, I said, "Glad you could start the tournament back up."

He dropped into the chair next to me. "Me too. That would have been quite an insurance payout if it didn't happen."

"Insurance?"

"Yeah. We always take out insurance in case there's any reason we can't continue the tournament. The sponsors only pay up if we follow through." He sat forward and pointed to the main screen. "I still can't believe Maude is one of our top players."

"You never know, I guess." My thoughts were spinning to motives. Did the insurance payout have anything to do with Caden's death? Would Kenneth benefit if the tournament didn't go on? I couldn't see how. But maybe someone else would.

A roar emanated from the front of the room. Several boys vaulted from their seats, punching their arms in the air.

"Looks like Maude might have met her match," Kenneth said.

I very much doubted that, not putting it past her to toy with her opponent.

Maude stood, stretched, and winked at me.

"I better circulate, since it's half-time," Kenneth said and moved to the front of the room to chat with Maude. I pondered what her winning might do for the tournament. Would that draw older folks into the game? Would the younger players leave?

Hoping that wink was encouragement for progress in finding clues, I wandered around the back of the room to work out the stress. How long was it going to take to come up with actionable evidence?

Dexter stood and high-fived his friend. It warmed my heart to see him enjoying himself with something he loved to do. I smiled at the memories of the training session Maude held at my cottage with those kids. Her legacy would remain long after she left town.

A horn sounded over the loudspeaker. In unison, everyone sat to resume play. The first round was half over.

As the games progressed, I couldn't help but notice the tension building in the room. Maude was now winning with ease, but Dexter was struggling. His opponents were taking advantage of his nerves, landing hits and scoring twice as much as he was. I could see the frustration building inside him, and I wanted to go over and offer some words of comfort, but I knew better. This was his moment, his chance to prove himself as a gamer.

Maude caught my eye from the front row, and I could see the determination in her eyes. I knew she was up to something, but I couldn't figure out what. As the games continued, I noticed her sneaking glances at her phone, typing away in the chat. What was she up to?

Suddenly, the main screen flickered to life, and a message appeared on the screen. "Attention all players and spectators. We have received a credible threat that someone may attempt to disrupt the tournament.

As a precaution, we will pause the games and conduct a security sweep of the premises. Please remain in your seats until further notice."

80

CHAPTER FOURTEEN

Panic set in as everyone scrambled to figure out what was happening. I could see Dexter and his friends huddled together, fear etched on their faces. Maude, on the other hand, looked unfazed, almost as if this was all part of her plan.

As we waited for further instructions, I was hopeful Maude and Barney had uncovered some reliable clues. Barney made his way to the front of the room for a quick huddle with Maude. He broke away and grabbed a microphone. Kenneth held a hand up and said, "Please let me have your attention," and handed the microphone to Barney.

The chatter immediately stopped, all eyes toward the front of the room. Was this all part of the plan to catch the killer?

Barney continued, "Our team is almost done. Please be patient."

"Will we be able to keep playing?" came a question from the crowd.

Barney looked at Kenneth and took a step forward toward the group. "We're doing everything we can."

Dexter had slumped into his chair, his head in his hands, appearing defeated.

I scanned the room, willing the killer to show. Were any of us in danger? If they felt the authorities were closing in on them, would they become desperate? Or worse, dangerous? They had already killed Caden. What would they have to lose by taking other people out?

Maude headed down the aisle toward me at the back of the room. She held out her phone. "I think I know who killed Caden," she said, her eyes meeting mine.

My heart raced as I waited for her to continue.

"I'm not sure if Kenneth is involved," she said, her voice barely above a whisper. "But I'm pretty sure Ian is. I've been monitoring his online activity, and I found some suspicious messages. He's been in contact with someone who goes by the name of TackleTitan."

Cupping my hand over my mouth, I bent close to her ear. "Do you think that's someone in this room?"

"Not necessarily. I have Steph checking out a few leads. I should know shortly."

"So, Barney is just stalling with this ruse?" I asked. That maneuver was a gamble if the killer got wind of it. I tapped my hands on my thighs, attempting to work out the nerves.

Barney's booming voice came over the speaker. "OK. We've been given the all-clear. You're free to resume." That was it. No details. The kids were all too eager to move on for the rest of their games.

Maude hustled with the energy of one of her teen opponents to return to her seat.

"Wow, this is wild, isn't it?" Ian, the tournament sponsor, stood next to me, his arms crossed. He pulled out his phone, the screen angled away from me.

The tenor of the room quickly settled as the second half of the games began.

Across the room, Dexter looked more determined than ever, rallying to score several times and take the lead over his opponent. Maude, however, seemed distracted, her focus now on her phone instead of the game. Her opponent had taken the lead at the two-minute warning. Was she genuinely going to lose or was this a strategy move?

"Finally," Ian muttered, pointing at the big screen.

"What?" I asked.

He shook his head. "So tired of seeing that old biddy taking over the game from these kids."

Wow! You would think he would be grateful for the publicity she was bringing to his company.

"Now, that's what I really want to see." He moved his arm in Dexter's direction. "He's a real up-and-comer."

Was he looking for a winner he could manipulate? If Dexter won, would he become a pawn for Ian? I worried now that Dexter was about to become embroiled in something larger than life that might seriously jeopardize his future.

Maude buried her head in her phone. She appeared willing to forego the victory in favor of what had her attention. She glanced at me and slightly shook her head. What did that mean? Did Steph's research lead to a dead end? Would the tournament end without catching Caden's killer?

Dexter's game had seconds to go. He was up by a touchdown. The other team had the ball near Dexter's end zone. He only needed to hold on a couple more plays to make it to the next round.

I clenched my fists, wanting to get some pom-poms and cheer him on.

The game on the main screen ended. Maude had lost. I only hoped it was to sacrifice for the investigation. "Yes!" Ian exclaimed.

Maude was completely consumed with texting, as my phone buzzed. She instructed me not to react. I waited for her next text. What seemed like minutes, but was only seconds later, she revealed the clues and the killer. He was standing just feet away from me.

The uproar at the front of the room consumed everyone's attention. Ian slunk over near Dexter as the game clock ticked to zero. Dexter had done it. He was going on to the next round. Leaping a foot in the air, he was met with chest bumps and high fives, including Ian.

I had to get between them. "Dexter," I said, waving him over to me. "Congratulations!"

He looked up at me, his eyes tearing up. "It's not about winning," he said. "It's about proving to everyone that I'm not just some kid who plays video games all day."

I nodded in understanding. "You proved that to me a long time ago," I said. "Don't let anyone else's opinion define you."

He smiled weakly and turned toward Ian as he joined us. "Thanks, Tilly. I appreciate it."

"Can't wait to see you go all the way," Ian said, slapping Dexter on the back.

From over Ian's shoulder, I saw Barney coming our way. He had his hand over his handcuffs that dangled from his hip. Ian was about to be taken into custody. I was ready to whisk Dexter aside to avoid any confrontation.

Ian followed my gaze and spotted Barney. He glared at me. "What did you do?"

Bewilderment covered Dexter's face. "Tilly? What's going on?"

Ian's eyes were wild as he barreled past me, his feet pounding the floor like a racehorse. He tucked his head low and took an abrupt turn around the last row of chairs, aiming for the exit.

Instead of a clean getaway, he tumbled into Florence as she carried the remaining cakes on her tray. He scrambled to get out from under her as she reared back and whaled on him with her tray. Holding his arms up to defend himself, Florence caused enough of a delay for Barney to join them. He jerked Ian up and pulled his arm behind his back, snapping the cuffs on him.

"Are you OK?" Barney asked Florence as she stood up.

"I am now." She scowled at Ian.

Rushing forward, I picked up the scattered cakes and placed them on the tray. Smiling at Florence, I said, "He might just have to deputize you."

She chuckled, "There's more to me than meets the eye." I was quickly learning that with Florence.

As Ian was being led away, I turned to Dexter. "Caden's killer has been caught. You can relax now."

Dexter's mouth hung open in disbelief. "Ian? But he seemed so nice."

Maude joined us, still glued to her phone. "Steph just sent me a picture of TackleTitan," she said, holding up her phone. "It's Ian's twin brother."

She regaled us with the details Steph had uncovered. Ian and his brother were jealous of Caden. He had gotten the attention of some other sponsors. When Caden told Ian he was going to another sponsor, Ian threatened to out him for cheating. There was a fight, and Ian strangled Caden.

Dexter's face paled as he listened to Maude's explanation. "I can't believe it," he muttered.

Maude continued. "Steph also found evidence that Ian was planning to sabotage Dexter's game, but she was able to prevent it in time."

Dexter looked at us both, his eyes wide with disbelief. "Thank you," he said, his voice shaking. "Thank you both for everything."

Kenneth's voice came over the loudspeaker. Everyone stopped in their tracks to hear the announcement. The day was ending, but they would pick up where they left off tomorrow. And the tournament would finish the next weekend.

Dexter turned to me, a smile spreading across his face. "I can't believe it's over. Now I can finally enjoy the tournament without any worries."

I grinned back at him. "Well, you better enjoy it while it lasts. The competition is only going to get tougher from here on out."

Dexter's smile turned playfully mischievous. "Challenge accepted."

CHAPTER FIFTEEN

I practically sprinted to Unkie's antique shop. My future was looking up with the bakery customers returning and Dexter in the clear. Sadly, Caden getting murdered paved the way for Dexter to have an opportunity in the gaming industry. And with Maude's tutoring, he had a real shot at achieving his dream.

Bursting into the shop, I was eager to share my good news with Uncle Jack.

"Hey," he hollered from the back of the store.

I looked around. "Where's Justin?" He had mysteriously asked me to meet him here. Those two were in cahoots for something.

"Oh, he'll be here," Uncle Jack said, waving his arm. "Tell me about the tournament. I understand Florence was smack dab in the middle of taking down the killer."

"You don't have enough time for that story," I said, laughing. I'll never forget that scene. Florence's cakes flying, her flower dress and apron swirling around her, and Ian splayed out underneath her.

"I understand business has returned with a vengeance."

Eternally grateful to Florence for kick-starting the throngs of customers, we had to add a third shift of baking for now. Maude had texted me not to worry about the on-line reviews anymore. I didn't even want to know what shenanigans she and Steph did behind the scenes.

Glancing at my phone, I expected to see a text from Justin. He was rarely late, and I expected his arrangements had to do with a final meeting with his parents before they left town. With my stress significantly reduced, I hoped I could be myself with them.

"Tilly, it's fine. Just relax." Uncle Jack smiled. "We need to go."

"Go?"

He tucked my arm under his as we exited the shop. I wasn't sure what to think about this. Not keen on surprises, I needed some dull in my life about now.

Dusk had set in with the boardwalk lights illuminating our path. I expected he was escorting me to dinner at Fiona's. Was she in on this secrecy? We reached the end of the boardwalk and arrived at the kayak rental shop. Now I was completely confused.

"What's going on?" I looked at Unkie.

He gestured toward the gently lapping waves. I slapped my hand over my mouth as tears formed in my eyes, completely stunned at the scene before me.

Candles in paper bags were placed on the sand, creating an aisle that led to a crowd. Justin, his parents, Linda, Barney, Florence, and Fiona waited at the end.

Turning toward Unkie, I squeezed him tight. He escorted me down the aisle as tears continued down my cheeks. I looked around at everyone's faces to imprint this memory. Uncle Jack joined the crowd as Justin bent on one knee.

He took my hand and said, "Tilly, you are an amazing woman. I love everything about you."

The sun was setting behind Justin, bathing him in the evening's glow. He pulled a ring from his pocket.

"You could say this beach is where it all began."

I laughed, recalling our first outing together. I wasn't even sure it was a date. He shoved me off in a kayak without a paddle and without him inside, leading to him having to rescue me.

"I can't think of a more perfect location to ask you this. Will you be my wife and join me on a journey filled with love, adventure, and endless possibilities?"

He gently slipped a ring on my finger as the crowd cheered. Standing up, he kissed me.

"Well?" he chuckled.

"Yes. Yes. A million times, yes."

The group surrounded us with congratulations and best wishes. I looked toward Justin's parents to gauge their reaction. We hadn't started on the right foot. Albert handed Patricia a hanky as she teared up. They were all smiles.

Patricia stepped forward and hugged me. "Welcome to the family, Tilly. We couldn't be happier for you both."

Albert joined her and said, "Justin never stopped talking about you. I felt like we knew you before we even arrived in Belle Harbor."

"Dinner is on me tonight to celebrate," Fiona said. "And girl, we have a lot of wedding planning to do."

As we walked to Fiona's restaurant, my mind raced with excitement. I had just agreed to marry the man of my dreams, and I couldn't wait to start our lives together. Justin and I had been through so much already, and I knew that we were meant to be together.

Arriving at Fiona's, familiar smells of smoked meats and pastas greeted us. We sat down and ordered some celebratory drinks, toasting to our future together.

"So, have you thought about when you want to get married?" Florence asked, a twinkle in her eye.

I looked at Justin, who smiled back at me. "It'll take some time to plan, but soon?"

"Yes, soon," he said, taking my hand in his again. The warm touch of his skin comforted me.

"Wait!" I said. "I need to tell my parents the good news." I jumped up and sped outside, eager to share. With my mom three thousand miles away, I had no idea how we were going to plan this wedding. All I knew was that I wanted it to be simple with just a few friends and family.

I returned to the table, face flushed. "They're very excited for us and wished us the best."

"I can't believe we're engaged," I said, beaming at Justin.

"I know," he said, pulling me close. "I love you so much, Tilly."

The evening continued with food, drinks, and laughter. We talked about our plans and what kind of wedding we wanted. Justin's parents were thrilled to join the celebration and already started planning their trip to Belle Harbor for the wedding. I couldn't wait for them to meet my parents.

"Tilly, you helped so much when Jack and I got married, I really want to return the favor," Linda said. "I want this to be as stress free as possible."

I bowed my head and wept, my emotions overflowing.

"I know your mom will want to be involved, but I'm here to make your life easier," Linda continued. "And of course, I'll help manage the bakery for your honeymoon."

"And if I do say so, Hawaii was magical for our honeymoon," Unkie piped up.

I glanced at Justin, who said, "We can go anywhere in the world you want."

Across the table from me, Barney slipped an arm around Florence. From the beginning, I pegged them as an odd couple, but their relationship continued to grow deeper. Would those two be next in line for nuptials?

What's Next? Ladyfingers and Lies

Rival gardeners, long-held secrets, and floral facade...

The annual Parade of Patios is the highlight of the spring season in Belle Harbor, showcasing the residents' green thumbs and creative flair. As the parade reaches the grand home of the esteemed town council president, the atmosphere turns chilling when a blood-curdling scream pierces the air.

In the council president's backyard, amidst a tapestry of flowers, the crowd stumbles upon a lifeless body.

As the danger grows like a stubborn weed, Tilly must unearth the truth before she becomes the next victim ensnared in this deadly flower bed. Will her keen eye for detail and unwavering determination be enough to expose the twisted roots of this mystery? Or will Belle

Harbor's charming gardens forever hide the secrets of a killer?

About the Author

S ue Hollowell is a wife and empty nester with a lot of mom left over. Finding a lot of time on her hands, and as a lover of mystery novels, she began telling the story of a character who appeared in her head. And she hasn't looked back. She likes cake, and the more frosting the better!